A Masai Tale

Who's in Rabbit's House?

retold by Verna Aardema

pictures by Leo and Diane Dillon

Dial Books for Young Readers
New York

For Danny Dufford, my new grandson — his first book

Who's in Rabbit's House? has been adapted by Verna Aardema from a Masai tale, *The Long One*, which appears in her collection, *Tales for the Third Ear from Equatorial Africa* (originally published by E. P. Dutton, 1969, now out of print). Ms. Aardema has skillfully combined repetition of key phrases with authentic African ideophones to produce a rhythmic read-aloud text which preserves the essential flavor of an African tale.

The art for *Who's in Rabbit's House? A Masai Tale* was prepared in pastels and tempera. After the original drawing was traced down, pastels were applied to the background and then the foreground was painted in tempera. The full-color artwork was then camera-separated and printed in four colors.

Text copyright © 1969, 1977 by Verna Aardema
Pictures copyright © 1977 by Leo and Diane Dillon
All rights reserved. Library of Congress Catalog Card Number: 77-71514
First Pied Piper Printing 1979 / Printed in Hong Kong by South China Printing Co.
COBE   10 9 8 7 6
A Pied Piper Book is a registered trademark of Dial Books for Young Readers,
a division of Penguin Books USA Inc.
® TM 1,163,686 and ® TM 1,054,312
WHO'S IN RABBIT'S HOUSE? is published in a hardcover edition by
Dial Books for Young Readers, 375 Hudson Street, New York, New York 10014.
ISBN 0-8037-9549-1

In their illustrations Leo and Diane Dillon have created a fantastic and magical world in which they skillfully blend elements of African art with eastern and western theatrical traditions. The Dillons have presented the humorous folktale as a play, performed for their fellow villagers by Masai actors wearing animal masks. The hairstyles, costumes, jewelry, housing, and general terrain are all typical of the Masai; the masks, however, are the Dillons' own artistic invention. As the story unfolds, the masks change expressions, showing merriment, horror, astonishment, in a way that could only happen in the realm of fantasy.

The opening pages of the book set the scene as the expectant onlookers gather before the drawn curtain. Then, as the play begins, the perspective shifts and the reader becomes the real audience to this unique performance.

As the hour for the performance approaches, the Masai villagers gather before the closed curtain, waiting expectantly.

Behind the curtain the actors prepare the set and the props, rehearse their lines, and don their masks.

At last the players are ready.
The curtain opens
and the play begins....

Long, long ago a rabbit lived on a bluff overlooking a lake.
A path went by her door and down the bank to the water.
The animals of the forest used that path when they went to
the lake to drink.

Every day, at dusk, Rabbit sat in her doorway and watched
them.

But one evening she came to her house and she could not get in.

And a big, bad voice from inside the house roared, "I am The Long One. I eat trees and trample on elephants. Go away! Or I will trample on you!"

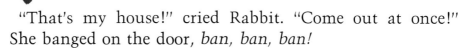

"That's my house!" cried Rabbit. "Come out at once!"
She banged on the door, *ban, ban, ban!*

But the bad animal said more crossly than before, "Go
away! Or I will trample on you!" And the rabbit sat
down on a nearby log to think.

Now a frog happened to see this. She hopped up to the rabbit and said rather timidly, "I think I could get him out."

"*Nuh!*" sniffed the rabbit. "You are so small. You think you could do what I cannot? You annoy me! Go away!"

Frog would have left that rude rabbit if a jackal had not come along just then.

Instead she crouched—*semm*—behind a nearby tree to see what would happen.

The jackal said, "Ho, Rabbit, why aren't you sitting in your doorway?"

"Someone's in my house," said the rabbit. "He won't come out. And I can't get in."

Jackal looked at the little house. "Who's in Rabbit's house?" he asked.

The bad voice replied, "I am The Long One. I eat trees and trample on elephants. Go away! Or I will trample on you!"

"I'm going!" cried Jackal. And off he went—*kpidu, kpidu, kpidu.*

The frog laughed softly to herself.

Rabbit cried, "Jackal, come back! Please help me!"

The jackal came back. He said, "I think I know what to do. We must gather a big pile of sticks."

They did.

"Now," said Jackal, "we'll put the sticks close to the house. Like this." And *kabak,* he pushed the whole pile of sticks against the door.

"But, Jackal," protested the rabbit, "that will keep him in! Not get him out!"

At that the frog nearly burst with mirth.

Jackal said, "I'm going to set fire to the sticks."

"Fire!" cried the rabbit. "That would burn my house!"

"It would burn The Long One too!" said Jackal.

"I won't let you burn my house!" cried Rabbit. "Go away!"
So the jackal trotted off *kpata, kpata* down to the lake.
Rabbit began to pick up the sticks. A leopard came by.
"What are you doing, Rabbit?" he asked. "Are you putting
sticks there to hide your house?"

"No, not that!" cried the rabbit. "Someone's in my house. Jackal wanted to burn him out. Now I have to take this wood away."

Leopard watched as Rabbit removed the sticks. Then he asked, "Who's in Rabbit's house?"

The bad voice said, "I am The Long One. I eat trees and trample on elephants. Go away! Or I will trample on you!"

"Nn-huu!" snorted the leopard. "You don't scare me! I'm tough! I'll tear that house to bits and eat you up!" And he leaped on top of the little house and began to scratch, scratch, scratch. Bits of the roof went flying—*zzt, zzt, zzt.*

"Stop!" cried the rabbit. "Don't spoil my house!"

"How can you use it—with a bad animal in it?" asked Leopard.

"But it's still my house!" said Rabbit. "Go away!"

So the leopard jumped down. And *pa, pa, pa* he went down to the lake.

And the frog grinned and chuckled to herself.

Rabbit climbed onto her roof. She smoothed and patted it —*bet, bet, bet!*

An elephant came by. "What happened, Rabbit?" she asked. "Does your roof leak?"

"No, not that!" cried the rabbit. "Someone's in my house. Leopard wanted to tear it to bits and eat him. So I had to fix my roof." She gave the roof another pat and hopped down.

"Who's in Rabbit's house?" demanded the elephant.

The bad voice said, "I am The Long One. I eat trees and trample on elephants. Go away! Or I will trample on you!"

"Trample on elephants?" sneered the elephant. "Who thinks he tramples on elephants! I'll trample you flat! Flat as a mat! I'll trample you—house and all!"

Gumm, gumm, gumm went Elephant toward the little house.

Rabbit leaped in front of her. "Don't smash my house!" she screamed.

"I'm only trying to help," said the elephant.

Rabbit said, "I don't want that kind of help. Go away!"

So the elephant tramped off *gumm, gumm, gumm* down to the lake.

And the frog laughed aloud—*gdung, gdung, gdung.*

"Stop laughing, Frog," said the rabbit. "See what that stupid elephant did to my yard. Now I have to smooth it." She found her hoe and set to work. *Kok, kok,* went the hoe.

A rhinoceros came by. He asked, "What are you doing, Rabbit? Are you making a farm here by your house?"

Rabbit stamped her foot. "No, not that!" she cried. "Someone's in my house. Elephant wanted to trample him. She made holes in my yard!"

"Who's in Rabbit's house?" asked the rhinoceros.

The bad voice said, "I am The Long One. I eat trees and trample on elephants. Go away! Or I will trample on you!"

"*Fuuuu!*" fumed the rhinoceros. "I'll hook you on my horn and hoist you into the lake—house and all!" He put his head down and *ras, ras, ras* he went toward the little house. But the rabbit leaped onto his nose. She held his big horn with her little paws.

Rhinoceros tossed his head. Up and away went Rabbit— *WEO* over the lake! Then—*NGISH!*

The rhinoceros shook himself in a satisfied way. "That's the end of The Long One," he said.

"But that was RABBIT you threw into the lake!" protested Frog.

Rhinoceros looked. The little house was not gone. But the rabbit was! The two rushed *pamdal* down the bluff to save Rabbit.

Now when the rabbit hit the water, she went *dilak, dilak, dilak* to the bottom of the lake. She kicked, and up she popped to the surface.

Elephant was still drinking at the lake. She saw the rabbit come up. "Keep kicking!" she called. She swam out and put her trunk around the rabbit and carried her to shore. "I saved you," she said. "But I don't know why. You are nothing but a bother!"

"Thank you, Elephant," said Rabbit. Then she went up the hill to her house. But she still could not get in. She sat on the log and began to cry—*wolu, wolu, wolu.*

The frog came up from the lake. "Don't cry, Rabbit," she said. "I think I could get that bad animal out of your house —if you would let me try."

"How?" asked the rabbit.

Frog whispered, "Scare him out."

Rabbit whispered back, "But how?"

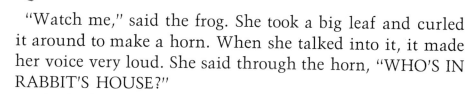

"Watch me," said the frog. She took a big leaf and curled it around to make a horn. When she talked into it, it made her voice very loud. She said through the horn, "WHO'S IN RABBIT'S HOUSE?"

The bad voice said, "I am The Long One. I eat trees and trample on elephants. Go away! Or I will trample on you!"

Frog said, "I am the spitting cobra! I can blind you with my poison! Now come out of that house, or I'll squeeze under the door and spit poison *SSIH* into your eyes!"

Then *hirrrr* the door opened.

Out came a long green caterpillar. He was so scared, his legs were jumping *vityo, vityo, vityo.* He was looking everywhere—*rim, rim, rim.* "Where's the spitting cobra?" he cried. "Don't let the spitting cobra get me! I was only playing a joke!"

"It's only a caterpillar!" cried Rabbit.

"Only a caterpillar," echoed Frog. She called the other animals. How they laughed when they saw that the bad animal was only a caterpillar.

But The Long One did not laugh. He was still saying,
"WHERE'S the spitting cobra? WHERE'S the spitting cobra?"

And Rabbit said, "Oh, Long One, the spitting cobra was
only Frog!"

At that Frog laughed so hard, all one could see of her was
her big laugh.

Then the big animals went away.
The Long One crawled up a tree.
Rabbit sat in her doorway.
   And the frog sat on the log croaking with laughter—
gdung, gdung, gdung.

The End